DRAGON MASTERS

POWER OF THE FIRE DRAGON

BY

TRACEY WEST

ILLUSTRATED BY

GRAHAM HOWELLS

BRANCHES

SCHOLASTIC INC.

DRAGON MASTERS
Read All the Books

TABLE OF CONTENTS

1. HOLD YOUR FIRE! 1
2. THE DRAGON SHOW 9
3. WHAT ABOUT WORM? 18
4. A WIZARD FOR A BABYSITTER .. 22
5. BEHOLD, THE DRAGONS! 29
6. TROUBLE IN THE TOWER 36
7. GUARDING THE CASTLE 41
8. THE HYDRA 46
9. MALDRED'S PLAN 55
10. RORI TO THE RESCUE 60
11. THE RED DRAGON STONE! 65
12. *POOF!* 72
13. THE QUEEN'S SURPRISE 78
14. A NEW DRAGON? 83

FOR MY NEPHEWS DANIEL AND COLIN,
who would be excellent Dragon Masters. –TW

Text copyright © 2015 by Tracey West
Interior illustrations copyright © 2015 by Scholastic Inc.

Library of Congress Cataloging-in-Publication Data
West, Tracey, 1965- author.
Power of the fire dragon / by Tracey West ; illustrated by Graham Howells.
pages cm. — (Dragon masters ; 4)
Summary: When the king decides to take the dragons to Arkwood to visit Queen Rose, Rori, Drake and their dragons are left behind — so when the evil wizard Maldred attacks the castle riding a giant four-headed dragon that spits poison, the two young dragon masters and their dragons are forced to defend the castle by themselves.
ISBN 0-545-64631-6 (pbk.) — ISBN 0-545-64632-4 (hardcover) — ISBN 0-545-64636-7 (ebook) — ISBN 0-545-75484-4 (eba ebook) 1. Dragons — Juvenile fiction. 2. Wizards — Juvenile fiction. 3. Magic — Juvenile fiction. 4. Adventure stories. [1. Dragons — Fiction. 2. Wizards — Fiction. 3. Magic — Fiction. 4. Adventure and adventurers — Fiction.] I. Howells, Graham, illustrator. II. Title. III. Series: West, Tracey, 1965- Dragon Masters ; 4.
PZ7.W51937Pntp 2015
813.54 — dc23
[Fic] 2014033958

ISBN : 978-93-8631-303-4

First printing, August 2015

This reprint edition, December 2022

Illustrated by Graham Howells
Edited by Katie Carella
Book design by Jessica Meltzer
Printed in India

HOLD YOUR FIRE!

"Vulcan, no!" Rori yelled.

Her big, red dragon shot fire from his mouth. The fire hit a bush. The bush burst into flames.

"Shu, quickly!" Bo called out.

A blue dragon darted through the air. A stream of water flowed from her mouth onto the fire.

"Thank you, Shu," said Bo, petting his Water Dragon.

"Vulcan," Rori said to her dragon. "I said to hold your fire!"

"Maybe he only heard *fire*," said Drake, trying to be helpful.

Drake was eight years old, and a Dragon Master. His friends Rori, Bo, and Ana were Dragon Masters, too. A magic stone called the Dragon Stone had chosen them. And each of them had a dragon to care for and train.

Today all four Dragon Masters and their dragons were in the Valley of Clouds behind King Roland's castle. They were getting ready for a special event.

"Rori, you must keep Vulcan under control," warned Griffith, the wizard who trained the Dragon Masters. He turned to the others. "King Roland will be here soon. He wants to see what your dragons can do."

"Is he really going to take us — and our dragons — to the Kingdom of Arkwood?" asked Ana. Her dark eyes were shining. "I've heard that Queen Rose's summer festival is wonderful."

"Yes," Griffith replied. "The king plans to show off the dragons at the festival."

"Then the dragons won't be a secret any longer!" said Drake. "We can finally tell our families about them."

"And everyone will see what an amazing dragon Vulcan is!" Rori added.

Griffith looked worried.

"What's wrong, Griffith?" asked Ana.

"I do not know if it is safe to bring the dragons out," he replied. "I tried to tell King Roland about Maldred the dark wizard. I told him that Maldred might be planning to attack. The king just laughed and said he was not afraid of any old wizard."

"But Maldred is dangerous!" Drake said. "He spied on us! His dark magic made Kepri sick! *And* he almost stole the Dragon Stone!"

Griffith nodded. "I know."

Rori balled up her fists. "If Maldred attacks, Vulcan and I will stop him! Vulcan is the strongest dragon ever!"

Bo looked at Drake and shook his head. Rori was always bragging about Vulcan.

"You are brave, Rori," said Griffith. "But you and Vulcan have not made a connection yet. Until you do, you must be careful."

Rori's face got red, and she looked away. Each of the Dragon Masters wore a piece of the magical Dragon Stone. When they were connecting with their dragons, their stone glowed green.

Drake — like Bo and Ana — could hear his dragon's voice inside his head. But this had not happened to Rori yet. And Drake knew it bugged her to be last.

"We may not have connected yet," Rori said. "But that doesn't mean we couldn't fight Maldred if he attacked!"

Just then, a soldier walked into the valley. "All welcome King Roland the Bold!"

THE DRAGON SHOW

King Roland marched across the grass. He was a big man with red hair and a bushy beard. Six guards marched behind him.

"The dragons are looking fine, wizard," he said in his booming voice. He nodded at Worm. "Even that brown one."

The king has never seemed to like Worm,
Drake thought. *So what if he looks like a big,
brown worm? He is a powerful Earth Dragon!*

"I'm glad that you are pleased, Your Majesty,"
said Griffith.

"I am not pleased yet!" the king said. "I need
to see what these beasts can do. This is the first
time that I will show my dragon army to the
world. When we march into the Kingdom of
Arkwood, everyone will be amazed!"

Ana stepped forward. "They're not an army!
They're just dragons."

A guard glared at Ana. "Silence, girl!" he barked.

"They are more than just dragons," said the king. "When word gets out that my kingdom is protected by dragons, nobody will dare attack us."

Maldred might attack us, Drake thought. But he did not say that out loud. *If the king didn't listen to Griffith's warning, he won't listen to mine.*

Griffith clapped his hands. "Dragon Masters, let us show King Roland what you can do. Please line up!"

The Dragon Masters had practiced for days. Drake felt excited. He couldn't wait for King Roland to see Worm's powers!

Griffith turned to the king. "First, I would like to present Bo and Shu, his Water Dragon."

Bo stepped forward and bowed. Then he waved his hand at Shu.

Shu floated in the air above them. Her blue scales shimmered. She opened her mouth and a stream of water came out. It flowed in a circle around them all. Then the water turned into misty droplets and fell to the ground.

King Roland nodded, smiling.

"And now, I present Ana and Kepri, her Sun Dragon," Griffith announced.

Ana climbed onto Kepri and sat in the saddle. She patted her neck. Then the slim, white dragon flew up into the sky.

Kepri did what she did best: She swirled and looped in the air. On her way down, Shu sprayed misty water into the air. Kepri sent a sunbeam out of her mouth. Together, they made a rainbow.

"*Ooohhhhh,*" said the guards. Even King Roland was staring in wonder.

"Rori and her Fire Dragon are next," said Griffith, pointing.

Drake was nervous. It would be his and Worm's turn soon. First, Vulcan would shoot fire in the air, where it couldn't hurt anything. Then Worm would use his mind powers to lift all three dragons in the air!

He watched as Rori and Vulcan flew up, up, up.

"Vulcan, fire!" Rori yelled.

Vulcan didn't listen. He flew down to the ground. When he landed, he let out a loud roar.

Whooosh! A stream of fire shot from his mouth! Then a strong wind blew through the valley.

"No, Vulcan!" Rori yelled.

The flame charged right at King Roland!

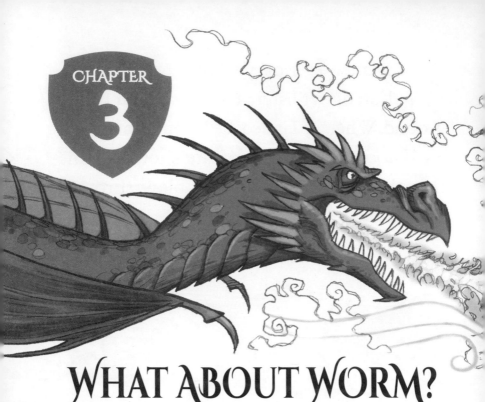

WHAT ABOUT WORM?

The fire rode the wind, closing in on King Roland. Scared, his guards all jumped back.

Suddenly, an invisible force knocked King Roland out of the fire's path. Drake looked at Worm. His dragon was glowing green. Drake knew that Worm had used his mind powers to save the king!

The fire swept past the king and died out.
Two guards helped King Roland to his feet.

"I am fine," he said, brushing them away.
Then he pointed at Vulcan. "No thanks to *this*
dragon!"

"But it was the wind!" Rori protested.

"Silence!" yelled King Roland. "I cannot have
this dragon setting Queen Rose's castle on fire."

He nodded toward Shu and Kepri. "I'll take these two."

"What about Worm?" Drake piped up. "He just saved you!"

"Saved me? I think not. One of my guards pushed me out of the way," the king said.

He looked at his guards. They all nodded.

"It wasn't a guard," Drake insisted.

He looked over at Ana and Bo. He could see they felt bad for him. Rori still looked mad about Vulcan.

"Drake speaks the truth, Your Majesty," Griffith said. "Worm moved you with the power of his mind."

"Impossible!" the king said. "This plain, brown dragon could not have such strange powers. Kepri and Shu will be the only dragons going to the Kingdom of Arkwood tomorrow."

The king turned and stomped away. His guards marched behind him.

Drake sighed, patting his dragon. "It's not fair," he said to Worm. "I know how great you are! Why won't the king believe us?"

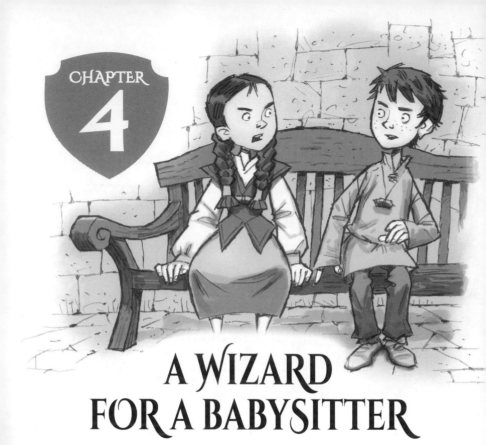

A WIZARD
FOR A BABYSITTER

top pushing me!" Rori shouted.

"I'm not pushing you!" Drake said, moving away from her on the bench.

It was the next morning. Griffith had asked Rori and Drake to sit quietly in the Training Room while the others got ready.

"Stop bickering, you two!" he said. "Stay out of trouble until Diego gets here. I will not leave for the Kingdom of Arkwood without another wizard here to watch over the castle."

Then Griffith went to help Bo and Ana with their dragons.

Sitting on the bench was boring. Drake kept squirming. And Rori kept complaining.

"Why does Diego have to come watch us?" she asked. "We don't need a babysitter."

"Well, maybe Griffith just wants to make sure that Vulcan doesn't set the castle on fire," Drake said. He knew it was kind of a mean thing to say. But Rori was really bugging him.

Rori's green eyes flared. "It was the wind!"

"Maybe, but Vulcan was supposed to shoot his fire high up in the air," Drake reminded her. "And because *you* can't control your dragon, Worm didn't get to show what he can do!"

Poof! The argument ended when a short, round wizard appeared in front of them.

"Rori and Drake! Good. Please come with me," Diego said.

They followed Diego to Griffith's workshop.

Diego pushed some papers off a table. He pulled a glass ball the size of a large onion from his pocket. Next, he put a circle-shaped stand on the table and rested the ball on it.

"Come, look in the gazing ball," he said, waving his hand over it. "Let's see what we can see."

"What are we looking for?" Rori asked.

"Some sign of Maldred," Diego replied.

"And his four-headed dragon?" Drake asked. "The one you saw in your dream the last time you were here?"

"Well—" Diego began. Rori interrupted him.

"But we don't even know what Maldred looks like," she pointed out.

Diego took a book from another pocket. He put it on the table and opened it to a page.

"*That's* Maldred," he said. Diego pointed to a picture of a wizard with a pointy chin. He wore an eye patch over his left eye. He had a black mustache and a long black beard with a white stripe.

"But I am not looking for Maldred's face in the gazing ball," Diego explained. "I am looking for a red mist — a sign of his dark magic."

Drake couldn't look away from the picture. The dark wizard seemed to stare at Drake right from the page. He was glad when Diego closed the book.

Rori and Drake crowded around to look in the gazing ball with Diego. There was no red mist. Just a white fog.

"Welcome, Diego!" Griffith called, walking into the workshop. "So should I be worried about Maldred while I am gone?"

"We should always be worried about Maldred," Diego replied. "But there is no sign of his magic in the gazing ball. And if anything happens, I will keep your Dragon Masters safe."

"I know you will, friend," said Griffith. Then he turned to Drake and Rori.

"Come!" he said. "It is time to see us off."

Griffith swept out of the room.

BEHOLD, THE DRAGONS!

They found Bo and Ana in the Training
Room, standing next to their dragons.

"Wow, you look so fancy!" Rori exclaimed.

Ana wore a yellow dress that shone like
the sun. Bo had on a silky blue tunic with a
wave design stitched into it. Shu and Kepri's
scales were clean and shiny.

Bo looked at Drake and gave a little bow.
"I will miss you, friend," he said.

"And I will miss you, too," Drake said. He
bowed back.

Ana squeezed Rori in a hug. "I wish you
could come!"

"Someone needs to stay here to guard the
castle," Rori said, trying not to show how sad
she really was. "It's an important job."

"Ana, Bo, it's time!" Griffith said.

Bo and Ana got onto their dragons. They waved as two of the king's guards led them out of the Training Room.

Drake and Rori jumped up. They quickly climbed to the top of the nearest tower so they could watch the parade.

"Wow!" Rori cried, looking down. "We can see all the way to my village from up here!"

Drake looked, too. A big crowd had come to the castle to see the dragons! His mother was probably down there.

Rori sighed. "I wish we were going, too."

"So do I," said Drake. *At least there's one thing Rori and I agree on!*

Then a trumpet blared loudly in the courtyard. "Behold, the dragons!" a guard announced.

Bo and Ana came out of the castle, riding Shu and Kepri, and the crowd gasped. King Roland nodded to them as he rode on his horse, leading the dragons. Rows of soldiers marched on either side. The crowd clapped and cheered as they left the kingdom.

Drake and Rori watched until the dragons were out of sight.

Suddenly, Rori pointed to Drake's Dragon Stone. Drake looked down. It was glowing green. Then he heard the voice of his dragon inside his head.

Trouble is coming!

Drake ran down the tower stairs, all the way to Worm's cave. Worm was sitting up. His eyes were bright green.

"What is it, Worm? What kind of trouble?" Drake asked.

Worm shook his head, like he wasn't sure.

Rori ran up behind Drake. "What's going on? What did Worm tell you?"

"He said trouble is coming," Drake replied. "But he doesn't know exactly what or when."

"Trouble, eh?" Diego said, walking into the cave. "*Hmm.* I haven't seen anything in the gazing ball. But Worm is good at sensing things. I can make a spell to find out if Maldred is blocking his magic so I cannot see it. I will get on it, so don't worry. Go have fun!"

But Drake found Diego's orders hard to follow. He could not stop worrying about Worm's message.

TROUBLE
IN THE TOWER

The next morning, the sun shone brightly through the window in Drake's room. He looked over at Bo's empty bed. It felt weird to be all alone.

When he got to the dining room, Rori and Diego were already eating breakfast. Drake sat down. Rori looked mad.

"No, Rori," said Diego, "you may not take Vulcan into the Valley of Clouds today."

"So, first, I could not go to Arkwood, and now, I cannot even go outside?!" asked Rori.

"The Valley of Clouds is too open. It may not be safe," said Diego. "But you may take Vulcan up to the tower."

"Yay!" Rori jumped up.

"If you see any danger, get right back inside the castle!" said Diego. Then he left to keep watch for any sign of Maldred.

"Let's go, Drake," said Rori.

She tapped her foot while Drake quickly finished his breakfast. Then they went down to the Dragon Caves.

Worm was still sleeping, so Drake didn't wake him.

He'll need his rest if trouble really is coming, Drake thought.

Rori ran to Vulcan's cave. He snorted happily when he saw her.

It was a tight squeeze in the stairway, but the big dragon followed Rori and Drake up to the tower.

As soon as they reached the balcony, Vulcan spread his wings. Then he launched off the balcony and flew up into the blue sky.

Rori smiled. "Look how amazing he is!"

Drake nodded. "Yes, he looks really strong."

"I know," Rori said proudly. "And Worm...
I know Worm can do amazing things, too."

It was the first time Rori had ever said
anything nice about Worm.

"Thanks," Drake said. "I think that Worm
is the right dragon for me. Just like Vulcan is
the right dragon for you."

Rori sighed. "I hope so. I just wish Vulcan
would connect with me."

Drake looked up at the sky. "I'm sure he
will soon."

Then he spotted something beyond Vulcan. "What's that?" he asked. He gasped. "Is that a dragon flying this way?"

Rori looked. "Maybe it's Shu or Kepri?"

But this dragon had green scales. And something else that made it different than their dragons.

"That dragon has four heads!" they both cried at once.

GUARDING THE CASTLE

The dragon swiftly flew toward the tower.

"Remember Diego's dream?" Drake asked. "He saw Maldred riding a four-headed dragon!"

Rori squinted. "There *is* a man on that dragon's back!"

Vulcan was still flying beside the tower. He hadn't seen the other dragon yet.

"Vulcan, come here!" Rori yelled. Her dragon circled back to the tower.

Curious, they watched as the strange dragon came closer. It had dark green scales. Each of the dragon's four long necks had lighter green scales. On top of each neck was a head with a short, thin snout that curved on the end like a beak.

Then they saw the man riding the dragon. He was wearing a red robe. He had an eye patch and a beard with a white stripe in it.

"It's Maldred!" Drake yelled.

Rori jumped on Vulcan's back.

"Rori, where are you going?" Drake asked.

"I'm going to fight Maldred!" she replied. "I'll show King Roland what Vulcan and I can do!"

"But Diego said we should get inside the castle! And we'll need Worm's help, too!" Drake said. "We can't fight Maldred on our own. He's too powerful!"

Rori wrapped her arms around Vulcan's neck. "This is *my* castle and *my* kingdom. I will stay and fight. You can go for help if you want," she said.

"Vulcan, let's go!" Rori cried.

Vulcan flew off the balcony. Drake knew he needed to get Diego and Worm up there quickly. Drake closed his eyes. He gripped his Dragon Stone.

Worm, come now! And bring Diego! he thought with all his might. *Please, Worm!*

Whoosh! A few seconds later, a green glow burst next to Drake. Worm and Diego instantly appeared on the tower.

"Drake, what's wrong?" Diego asked.

Drake pointed to the sky.

Rori and Vulcan were flying right toward Maldred and the four-headed dragon!

THE HYDRA

ulcan, fire!" Rori yelled.

Vulcan blasted the four-headed dragon with a stream of fire. The dragon swiftly soared up, avoiding the flames.

"The hydra from my dream!" Diego cried.

"Diego, I told Rori she can't fight Maldred on her own. But she wouldn't back down. She doesn't even have her saddle on! She could slip off Vulcan any minute!" Drake yelled.

"Oh, dear!" Diego cried. He pointed a finger at Vulcan.

Poof! A saddle appeared underneath Rori.

Rori looked surprised for a second. Then she grabbed onto the reins.

"Hi-yah!" she cried. Vulcan charged up toward the hydra.

The hydra opened all four mouths.

"Rori, steer away!" Diego yelled. "The hydra shoots poison!"

But Rori didn't listen. "Fire!" she yelled again. Vulcan shot out more flames just as the hydra attacked with a green mist. The fire and the mist met in midair.

ROOOOAAARR! Vulcan cried out as some of the mist hit his wing. Then he dove down to the ground toward safety. Rori held on tightly.

Diego rushed to the edge of the balcony.

"Maldred! Come over here and fight like a wizard!" Diego challenged.

Maldred turned at the sound of Diego's voice. He steered the hydra down to the balcony.

Drake ducked behind Worm. Up close, he could see that the hydra's eight eyes were glazed over red.

"I am not afraid of you, Diego! Your magic cannot stop me!" Maldred said. He stared right at Drake. "You are a Dragon Master, aren't you?"

Drake was too scared to answer.

"It was *your* dragon that destroyed my red orb," the wizard went on. "But your dragon's little trick revealed his powers to me."

"What do you know about Worm?" asked Drake.

"*Yarrrrrrgh!*" Diego let out a cry. "Begone!" He pointed at Maldred. Blue lightning shot from his finger. Smiling calmly, the evil wizard waved his hand. The blue lightning sizzled out in midair.

Maldred laughed. "Is that all you've got for me, wizard?"

Diego turned to Drake. "Maldred is much too powerful," he whispered. "We need Griffith. I'll use magic to get to him quickly. But, Drake, you must stay here. Use Worm to get Rori and Vulcan to safety!"

Drake nodded. "I will try."

Diego snapped his fingers and vanished.

Rori and Vulcan swooped down from the sky. The Fire Dragon's wing still sizzled from the poisonous attack. Maldred flew up high, back into attack position.

"Fire!" Rori yelled.

Vulcan blasted the hydra again. Then the hydra shot more poison at Vulcan. Vulcan dodged it, but it hit one of the castle towers. The stone sizzled and then started to melt!

Drake caught Rori's eye. She looked frozen in fear.

"Rori, fly down!" Drake called up to her. "Touch Worm! We need to get out of here!"

"I know this trick!" yelled Maldred. "You aren't going to vanish into thin air this time!" Then he pulled on the reins to make the hydra dart toward the tower.

Worm began to glow green. But Rori still wasn't moving. She would need to touch Worm so he could transport them all out of there.

"Come on, Rori!" Drake urged. Then he turned to Worm. "Worm, you'll need to float up there! Hurry! Touch Vulcan! And I'll jump up to touch your tail!"

Worm nodded. He began to float.

Then Drake heard an evil laugh. He turned and saw Maldred holding up a glowing, red stone. Red light shot out from the stone.

Startled, Vulcan bucked under Rori.

Zap! A beam of red light hit Worm right between the eyes. Drake stumbled backward as he watched Worm's eyes glaze over red—just like the hydra's eyes. Then the light formed a red bubble around Worm. The bubble floated toward Maldred.

"Worm! No!" Drake yelled.

Maldred grinned. "Worm is mine now!"

MALDRED'S PLAN

The red bubble holding Worm floated in the air beside the hydra.

Maldred aimed the red stone at Vulcan.

"Get him away, Rori!" yelled Drake.

Rori pulled hard on the reins just as the red beam of light came bursting out of the red stone. This time, Maldred's magic was a second too late. Vulcan had already shot up over the castle. Drake watched Vulcan and Rori fly out of sight.

He was all alone.

Did Rori leave me here? And when will Diego get back? he wondered. Sweat broke out on his skin.

"Let that big brute fly away," Maldred said. "Worm is the dragon I want. Worm is what I came for — he is my prize!"

Drake tried to contact Worm. He touched his Dragon Stone. *Worm, can you hear me? Are you okay?*

Worm didn't answer.

Suddenly, Drake didn't feel scared anymore. He felt angry.

"Leave Worm alone!" Drake yelled.

Maldred laughed. "You do not even know how truly powerful this dragon is. I have known since the day I sent my spy orb into your castle. I saw his powers then. I knew he was the only dragon I would need to carry out my plan."

"Worm is *my* dragon!" Drake called out bravely. "How can you control him without a Dragon Stone?"

Maldred held up the red stone. "This is a red Dragon Stone. Created by magic. Dark magic. With this stone, I can make any dragon follow my orders."

Drake looked at the red glaze in the hydra's eyes. *Of course! Maldred must have captured the hydra, too! And he's making it attack us. What kind of bad things will Maldred make Worm do?*

Drake got a bad feeling in his stomach.

"What do you need Worm for?" said Drake. "You already have a four-headed dragon by your side!"

Maldred grinned. "She is powerful, but not as powerful as Worm," the wizard replied. "Worm can move mountains. Worm can move armies. He can even make the earth shake. With this red Dragon Stone and Worm by my side, *all* kingdoms will bow down to me!"

"They'll never bow to you!" Drake yelled. But his whole body was shaking with fear. *Where is everybody?*

Unless help came fast, Maldred would win!

RORI TO THE RESCUE

Worm! *Can't you do something—anything— to stop Maldred?!* Drake thought. But Worm didn't answer.

"He's not yours! You can't take him!" Drake shouted at Maldred.

"Just watch me do it," Maldred said with an evil grin.

Drake watched helplessly as Maldred pulled on the hydra's reins. The hydra turned away from the tower. The wizard began to fly off, with Worm floating beside him.

Then Drake heard a loud roar. Vulcan came speeding through the air with Rori on his back. They had circled the castle!

Vulcan stopped at the tower.

"Climb on!" Rori yelled.

Drake swiftly got on the saddle behind Rori. He put his arms around her.

"Hurry!" Drake yelled as Vulcan took off.

Drake's stomach jumped. When he looked down, the ground was spinning.

"Vulcan, stop Maldred!" cried Rori.

Vulcan soared until he caught up with the hydra. Maldred slapped the reins against the hydra's back, spurring her to go faster.

But Vulcan was fast, too. He flew over the hydra's head.

Then he made a big upside-down loop in the air. Drake gripped Rori and closed his eyes tightly.

When he opened them, Vulcan was head-to-heads with the hydra.

Maldred glared at the Dragon Masters.

"You children are annoying me," he said. "Hydra!"

All four heads snapped to attention. Then all four mouths opened. Drake could see a green tornado swirling inside each one.

"Vulcan, fire!" Rori yelled.

"Make it big!" Drake added.

Before Vulcan could attack, Maldred pointed a finger at the dragon. Sizzling red lightning shot out and zapped Vulcan. The dragon froze in midair.

"Vulcan, fly!" Rori pleaded. But the dragon was like a big statue, floating in the air.

Drake looked down. He and Rori couldn't jump. They were too high up.

"Hydra, attack!" yelled Maldred.

THE RED
DRAGON STONE!

he hydra aimed all four heads at Drake
and Rori.

The poison will hit us! Drake thought. *It
melted stone!* He shivered.

Suddenly, a bright, white light filled the air.

Drake had to shield his eyes. He could hear the hydra squealing.

The light faded, and Drake looked up.

Ana and Kepri swooped down from the sky! Kepri was shining a sunbeam on the hydra.

The four-headed dragon thrashed around, confused. The poison tornadoes shot sharply to the left, missing Drake and Rori. Maldred lost his hold on the reins and scrambled to grab them.

Poof! Diego appeared on the tower.

"Diego! You did it!" Drake said happily.

"We came as fast as we could!" Diego said.

Then Shu swept in, carrying Bo and Griffith. She flew to the tower and Griffith jumped off to join Diego.

Shu can cure dark magic spells! Drake remembered. *She cured Emperor Song back in Bo's kingdom.*

"Bo, Maldred used dark magic on Vulcan!" Drake yelled. "Shu can heal him!"

Bo nodded and steered Shu down to Vulcan. The hydra was still squirming under the light of Kepri's sunbeam. Maldred struggled to control her. He couldn't stop Shu.

Bo whispered in Shu's ear. A misty blue cloud floated from her mouth. Then a light blue mist rained down on Vulcan's head. The mist shimmered in the air.

When the mist settled, Vulcan began to flap his wings.

"Vulcan, you're okay!" Rori cried.

Over on the tower, Diego and Griffith faced each other. Lightning shot from their fingertips, and a ball of blue energy began to form between them.

"We can defeat Maldred, but we need time!" Griffith called up to the Dragon Masters.

"Don't let him get away!" added Diego.

Maldred grabbed one of the reins. With his other hand, he shot a red beam at Kepri. Ana steered Kepri away, and the attack missed. But her sunbeam stopped, and the hydra started to calm down. Maldred held up the red stone.

"Rori, can you steer Vulcan next to the hydra?" Drake asked. "If we can destroy the red Dragon Stone, I think Worm and the hydra will be back to normal!"

"No problem!" Rori said. She steered Vulcan sharply to the left.

Maldred held out the red Dragon Stone. A beam shot out, headed right for Vulcan.

"Rori, look out!" Drake warned.

CHAPTER 12

POOF!

Rori pulled hard on Vulcan's reins, pulling him straight up. Drake's stomach lurched. The red beam zipped past them.

Vulcan dove back down like a hawk diving for prey. He flew so fast that Maldred couldn't have hit him if he tried.

"Now!" Rori yelled as they sped past Maldred.

Drake reached out and smacked the red Dragon Stone out of Maldred's hand. It flew through the air.

"No!" the evil wizard cried.

The Dragon Stone hit one of the towers and shattered into pieces.

"Yes!" Drake cheered.

Pop! The red bubble around Worm vanished. The red in his eyes slowly changed from red back to green. Drake glanced at the hydra. All eight of her eyes looked normal, too.

Worm turned to face Maldred. The dragon's eyes glowed green. Then his whole body began to glow.

Maldred floated up off the hydra's back. Worm used the power of his mind to keep Maldred floating in the air!

"Stop! I command you!" the wizard screamed as he dangled in midair.

The hydra's four heads looked around, confused. Then she flew away.

"The spell is ready now!" Griffith yelled. "Everyone get away from Maldred!"

The Dragon Masters quickly flew out of the way. The blue ball of energy between Griffith and Diego was the size of a small boulder. The wizards' hair stood on end.

They moved their arms, pushing the energy toward Maldred. The evil wizard looked angry as the ball of blue energy raced closer to him.

"This is not over! Nothing can hold *me*!" Maldred yelled. And then . . .

Poof! He disappeared.

Everyone moved to the tower. The dragons hovered above the two wizards.

"Did Maldred escape? Where did he go?" Drake asked.

"He did not escape. We sent Maldred to the Wizard's Council prison. It is quite magic-proof," Diego explained.

"I am very proud of all of you," Griffith said. "Drake and Rori especially. You defended the castle. King Roland will be told of your bravery."

"Oh, no! King Roland!" Ana cried. "He's going to be angry that we left Queen Rose's festival in such a hurry."

"That is true," Griffith agreed.

"Worm can get us there quickly!" Drake said. Then he paused. "That is, if Worm and Vulcan are invited now."

Griffith smiled. "Everyone touch Worm!" he said.

The Dragon Masters reached for Worm. Diego and Griffith touched him, too.

"Worm, take us to Queen Rose's castle!" Drake said.

Worm's body glowed green again.

Whoosh!

They all disappeared.

CHAPTER 13

THE QUEEN'S SURPRISE

The Dragon Masters, wizards, and dragons appeared in the courtyard of Queen Rose's castle. Drake's eyes got wide as he took in the amazing sight.

King Roland and Queen Rose sat at a head table. People from the Kingdom of Arkwood sat at other tables — all piled high with food.

Everyone gasped at the sight of the dragons. Then they began to clap and cheer.

"How wonderful!" Queen Rose cried as she stood up. "You tricked us, King Roland. I thought your dragons had left us. But that was just part of the surprise. They have returned with two *new* dragons!"

King Roland coughed. "Yes, that is exactly what I planned," he said. "Griffith, why don't you introduce our new dragons?"

Griffith stepped forward. "This is Worm," he said, pointing to the brown dragon. "Worm may not look strong, but his mind is powerful. He is the one who transported us from Bracken to here — all in the blink of an eye!"

Everyone clapped. Drake could hear the crowd whispering.

"And this is Vulcan," Griffith said, pointing. "Rori, show us what Vulcan can do — safely."

Rori nodded. "I can do that," she said, but her voice was shaking. Drake guessed she was nervous that Vulcan might not listen.

Suddenly, her Dragon
Stone began to glow.

Rori closed her eyes. "I
can hear Vulcan's voice
in my head!" she cried,
smiling. "It's happening!
We're finally connecting!"

Vulcan slowly stepped
into the center of the courtyard. A thin flame
streamed from his nostrils. One by one, he lit
up the candlesticks on each table.

Queen Rose clapped. "Wonderful! You are lucky to have such amazing dragons, King Roland. Thank you for sharing them with us today."

King Roland smiled. "They *are* amazing," he said proudly.

The Dragon Masters looked at one another and smiled.

Now everyone knows how special you are, Drake told Worm, and his dragon smiled.

A NEW DRAGON?

he next afternoon, the Dragon Masters
went to the Valley of Clouds for flying practice.
Before they could begin, King Roland marched
in with his guards.

"I must have a word with you all," he said
in his gruff voice.

Oh, no! Drake thought. *Is the king mad about us bringing Worm and Vulcan to see the queen? But he seemed so happy with us last night!*

"Griffith has told me of a great battle that happened yesterday," the king said. "A battle against a dark wizard and a four-headed beast."

"It wasn't a beast," Rori piped up. "That dragon didn't do anything wrong. The wizard *made* it attack us."

"Still, it was very brave of you all," the king said. "And I am grateful."

Drake could not believe his ears. *Is this really happening? Is the king thanking us?!*

"Tonight, I am throwing a big feast in your honor," King Roland went on. "Drake and Rori, I understand you have family in our kingdom. They will be invited."

"Yay!" Drake and Rori cheered.

"I may even invite Queen Rose," the king added. His cheeks got a little red. He coughed. "Since she is very fond of the dragons."

He turned to Griffith. "And you may invite that little round fellow who comes around."

"Thank you, Your Majesty," Griffith said. "Diego will be pleased."

"Yes, thank you!" the Dragon Masters said.

The king left, and everyone started talking at once.

"A feast!" cried Bo.

"I'll get to see my mom!" Drake cried.

"And my dad!" added Rori.

Suddenly, Bo pointed up to the sky. "What is that?"

The hydra was flying across the forest on the other side of the valley. The four-headed dragon swooped down and landed nearby.

"Oh, she looks sad," Ana said.

"Ana is right." Griffith said. "Come, let us see if the hydra needs our help."

Together, they slowly approached the dragon. Worm slithered ahead of everyone. He stood in front of the hydra for a moment. Then Drake heard Worm's voice in his head.

She is far from home, he said. *But her home is not safe. She would like to stay here.*

"Worm says she needs to stay with us," Drake told everyone. "Where she's from isn't safe."

"Worm told you all that?" Griffith asked.

Drake nodded. "Yes. I knew that Worm could talk to other dragons. But this is the first time he's shared their thoughts with me."

"So can the hydra stay?" Rori asked.

"Of course," Griffith said. "We will give her a cave of her very own."

The hydra slowly raised her four necks and stared at the Dragon Masters. Her eyes were a pretty yellow color.

Ana approached her and gently stroked her neck.

"I wonder what her name is?" Ana asked.

Griffith smiled. "That will be for her new Dragon Master to choose."

"A new Dragon Master!" said Drake. "Really?"

"Yes," Griffith said. "The Dragon Stone will choose one for us soon."

"I wonder who it will be?" Bo asked.

Drake smiled. "I can't wait to find out!"

TRACEY WEST was born with red hair like Rori's, and she can be just as bossy as Rori is sometimes. But Tracey wishes she could be as brave as Rori is, too! Doing upside-down loops on a Fire Dragon would make Tracey very queasy.

Tracey has written dozens of books for kids. She does her writing in the house she shares with her husband and three stepkids. She also has plenty of animal friends to keep her company. She has two dogs, seven chickens, and one cat, who sits on her desk when she writes! Thankfully, the cat does not weigh as much as a dragon.

GRAHAM HOWELLS lives with his wife and two sons in west Wales, a place full of castles, and legends of wizards and dragons.

There are many stories about the dragons of Wales. One story tells of a large, legless dragon—sort of like Worm! Graham's home is also near where Merlin the great wizard is said to lie asleep in a crystal cave.

Graham has illustrated several books. He has created artwork for film, television, and board games, too. Graham also writes stories for children. In 2009, he won the Tir Na N'Og award for *Merlin's Magical Creatures*.

DRAGON MASTERS
POWER OF THE FIRE DRAGON

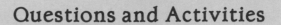

Questions and Activities

Why are only TWO of the dragons invited to Queen Rose's festival?

Why do you think Maldred is so interested in Worm? What might he do once Worm is under his control? Reread page 59 for clues.

How does Maldred control the dragons?

King Roland's voice is described as *booming* and *gruff*. Think of other similar **ADJECTIVES** to describe King Roland's voice. Use a dictionary or thesaurus for help!

Imagine you are the hydra's new Dragon Master. Write and draw pictures about your adventures. **SHARE** your story with a friend!

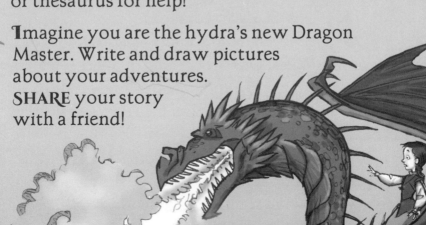